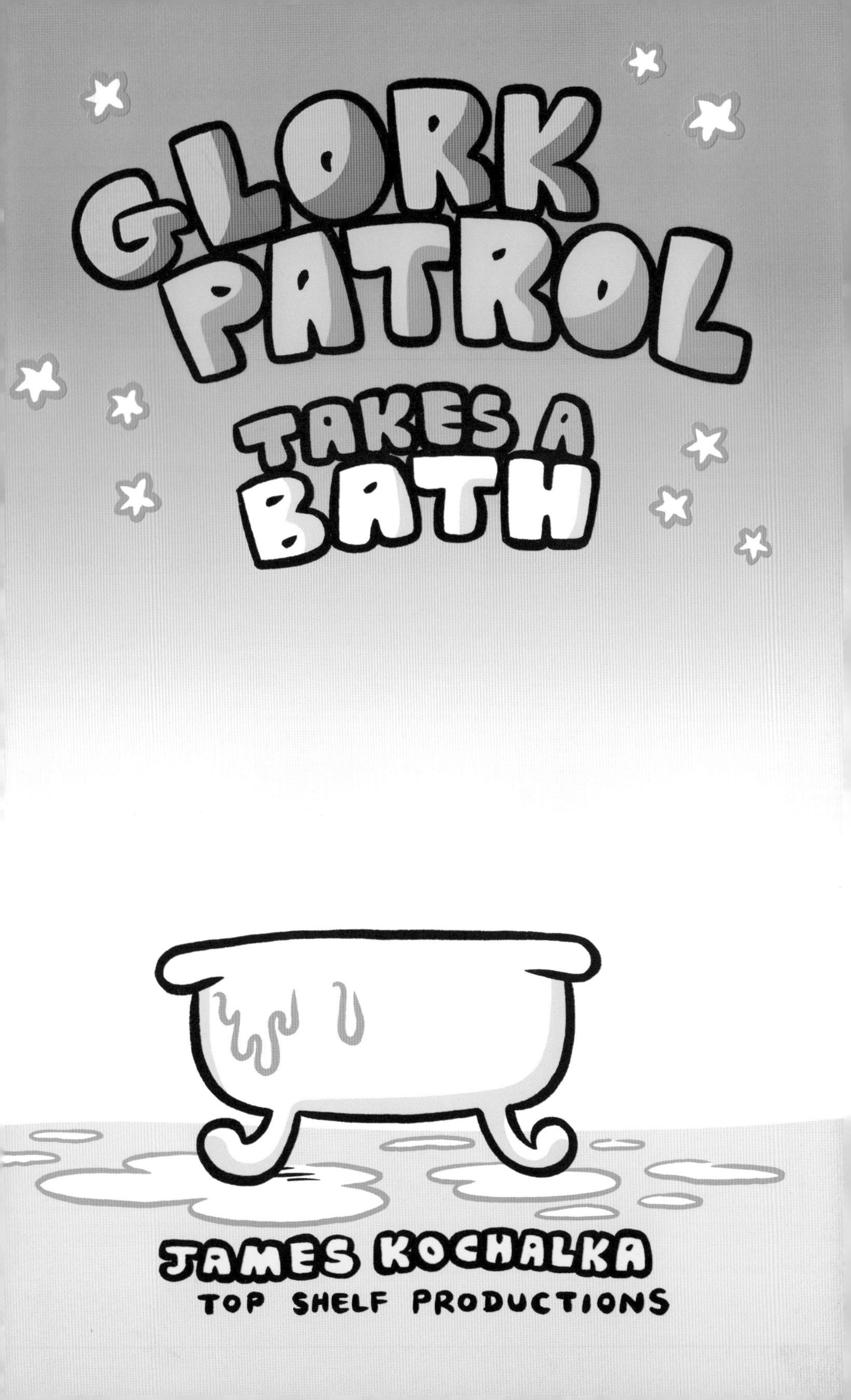
GLORK PATROL
TAKES A BATH
JAMES KOCHALKA
TOP SHELF PRODUCTIONS

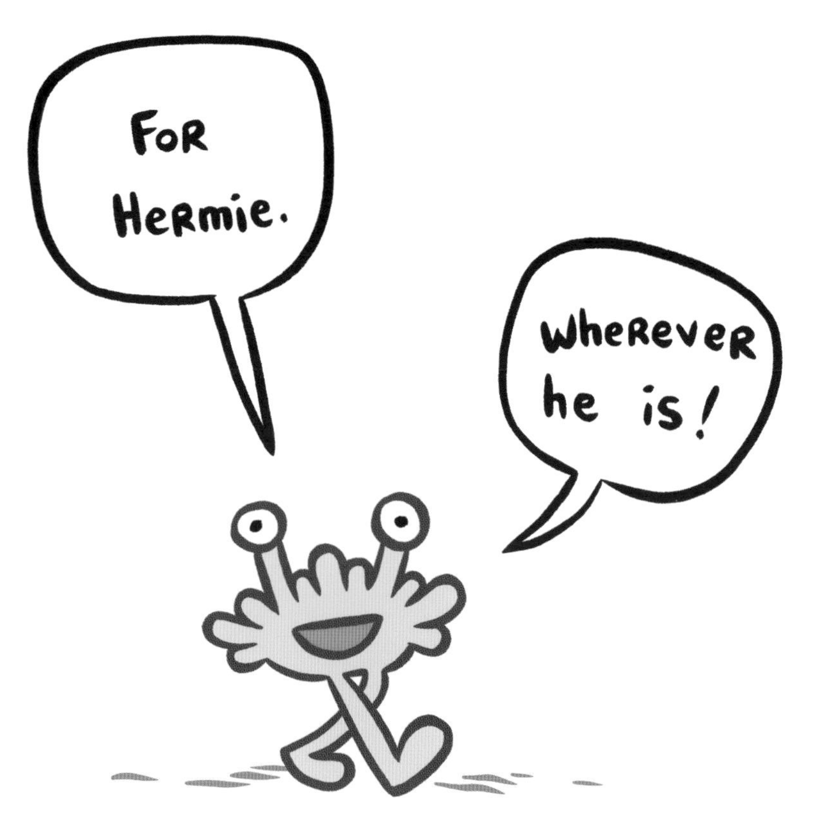
For Hermie.
Wherever he is!

ISBN 978-1-60309-504-4 26 25 24 23 22 1 2 3 4 5

Published by Top Shelf Productions, an imprint of IDW Publishing, a division of Idea and Design Works, LLC. Offices: Top Shelf Productions, c/o Idea & Design Works, LLC, 2765 Truxtun Road, San Diego, CA 92106. Top Shelf Productions®, the Top Shelf logo, Idea and Design Works®, and the IDW logo are registered trademarks of Idea and Design Works, LLC. 

Printed in China.

Editor-in-chief: Chris Staros.
Edited by Leigh Walton.
Designed by Nathan Widick.

Visit our online catalog
at topshelfcomix.com

Good morning, Glork Patrol!
Good morny, Glorkian Super Grandma!
Quack!

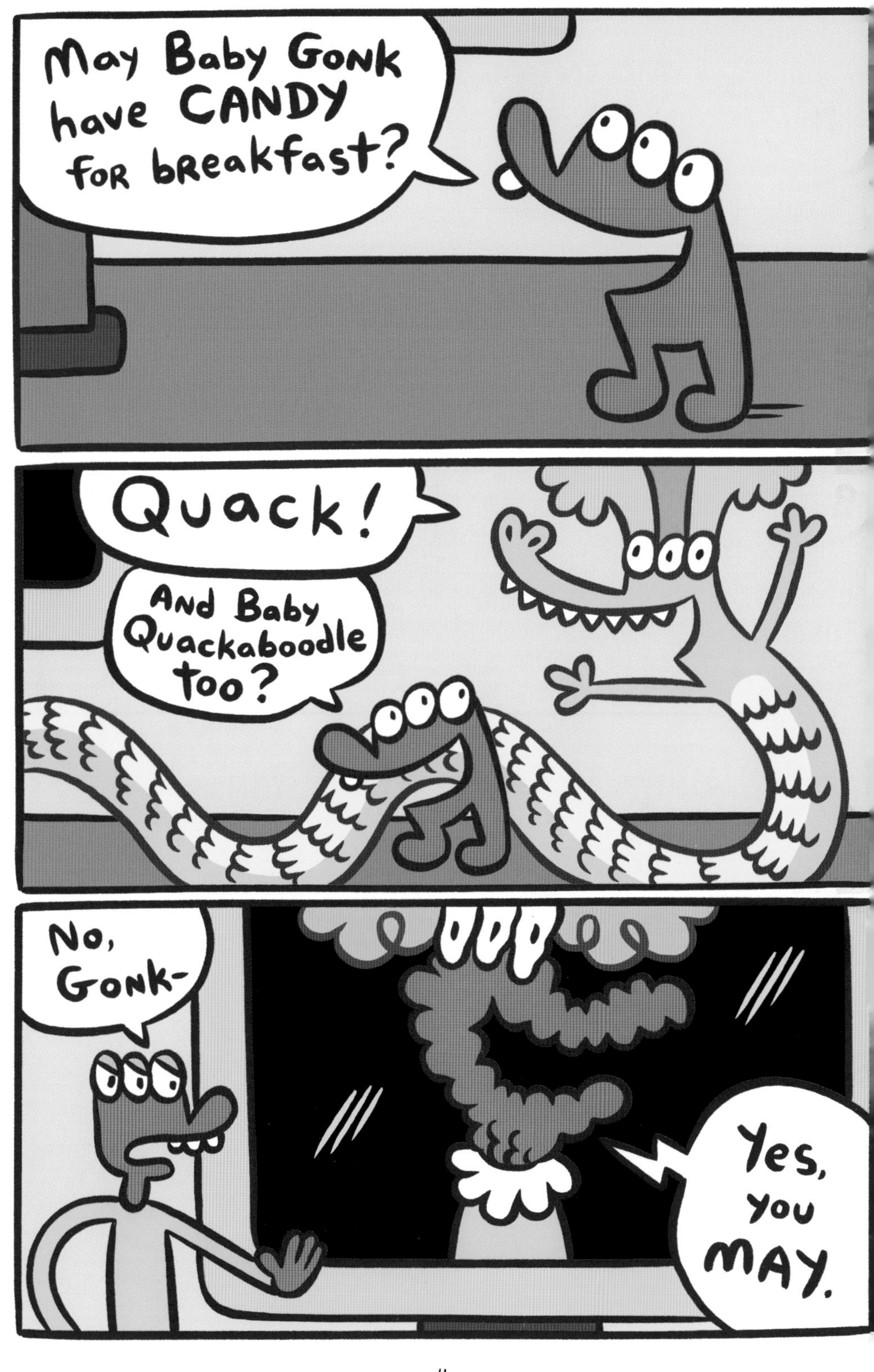
May Baby Gonk have CANDY for breakfast?
Quack!
And Baby Quackaboodle too?
No, Gonk-
Yes, you MAY.

HOORAY!
slither!
Thank you, Super Grandma!
But... but...
Candy for breakfast?
Can I have candy too?
No, you may not, darling.
Aw! No fair!

I have a very important BIG BOY mission for YOU.
You do?
Wow!
I'm special!
Glorkian Warrior, reporting for DUTY, Super Grandma.
SALUTE!
I'm Ready for ANYTHING.
Good, good! Now, don't forget your Super Backpack, dear.
Oh, yeah!

Here I am, Boss.
Waiting in my little bed.
I found you!
I wear you on all my most dangerous missions!
I know, Boss.
Okay, Super Grandma! I'm READY NOW!
What is my mission?
Thump
It's time to go on Glork Patrol.
What, again?
I did that LAST time.

Now, now, Dearie. You know...
"A Glork Patrol a day keeps DISASTER away."
I know, I know. It's just so BORING.
You can do it, Boss.
I believe in you!
That's a good Super Backpack.
Make sure he does his job!
I will, Grandma.
Hmph.
Glorkian Super Grandma, over and out!
Bye-bye!
BLINK

Another Glork Patrol, Boss! What fun!
Ugh.
Whatever.
Hey... what's all this trash?
Looks like candy wrappers.
GONK! Why is TRASH on the FLOOR?
Me don't know, Da-da! But look how HAPPY we am!
Quack!

Also, guess what else!
Gonk teach Baby Quackaboodle to TALK.
Her can say CANDY now:
Quacky!
Me teach her that.

Now YOU teach a WORD, Da-da!
Quacky?
Quacky? Quacky? Quacky?
GRRRR!
TWITCH!
Look! Look! Da-da am getting READY to teach a WORD!
SHAKE! TWITCH!
Quacky?
Quacky quack?

No!
DA-DA! NO am a BAD WORD!
Eeep!
You SCARE her!
No!
No! No! No!
WUMP
I don't wanna go on GLORK PATROL again!
KICK KICK
I don't wanna! I don't WANNA!
KICK KICK KICK!

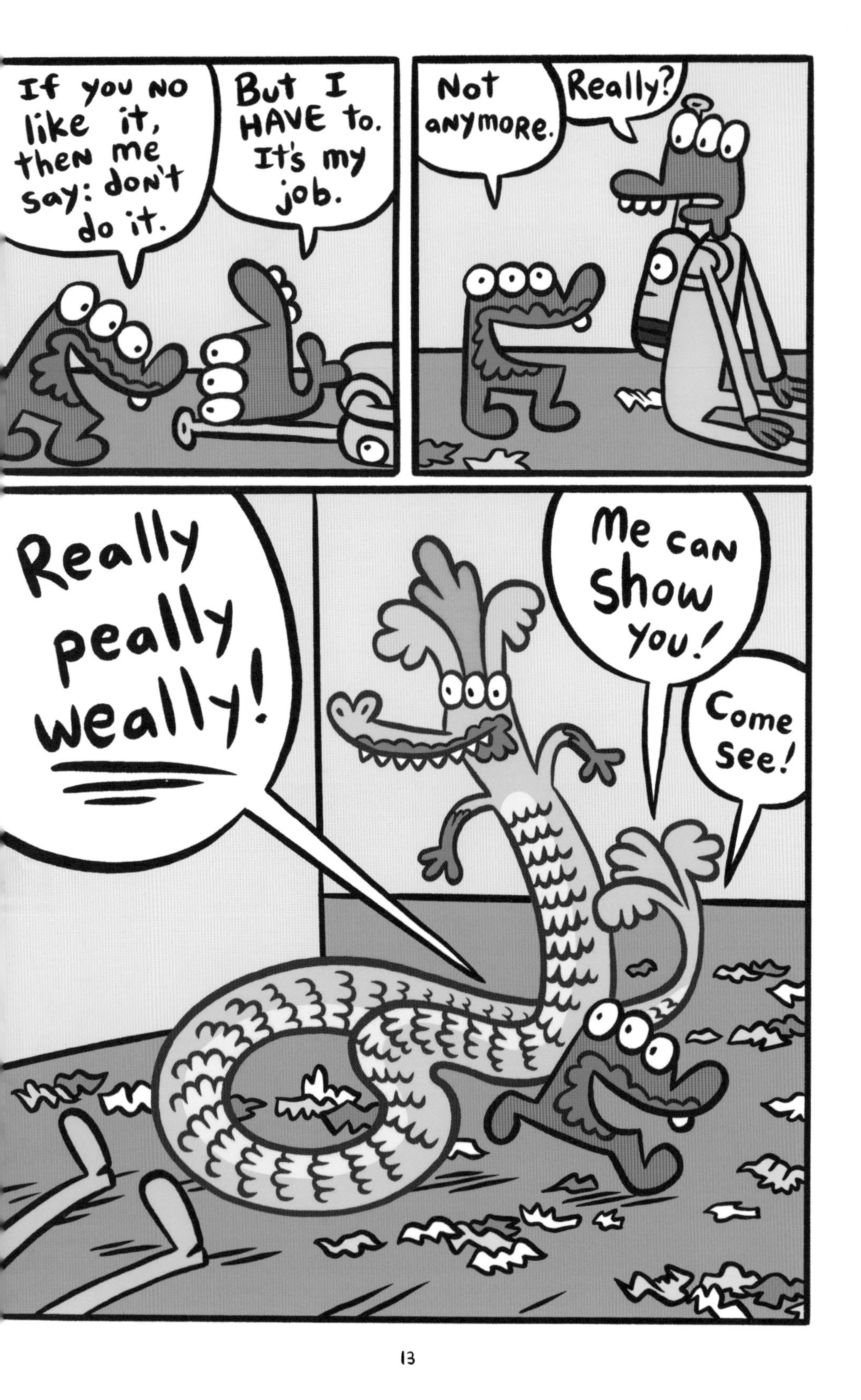
If you NO like it, then me say: don't do it.
But I HAVE to. It's my job.
Not anymore.
Really?
Really peally weally!
Me can show you!
Come see!

Up up uppy the stairs!
See, Da-da?
Look!
It am a Robo-suit! For Super Backpack!
Quack!
Put them IN!

IN!
Yeah, Boss! Put me IN.
Okay...
I always wanted my own ROBO-SUIT.
Yay!
CLICK
This is going to be so COOL!

See, Da-da? Now Super Backpack can do Glork Patrolies for you.

Yes!

Also, now I can do this:

TA-DA!

Wow.

But...
How did little kids get the MONEY to buy an expensive ROBO-SUIT like that?
We DIDN'T buy it.
Right?
We MADE the WHOLE THING from CANDY WRAPPERS!
QUACK!
And Gum!

Well... goodbye, everyone.
I'm going on GLORK PATROL now.
I'll be back SOON.
WAIT!
Waity WAIT!
Huh?
YOU need backpack!
Quack!
Strap ME on you!

Quack!
See? Me can be Super Gonkpack for YOU.
Thanks, Baby Gonk! You're right.
I do need one.
Bye-bye, Da-da! Have nice time on DAY OFF.
Take good care of Baby Quackaboodle while me am gone.
Me love you!
This GLORK PATROL is going to be AWESOME!

WAVE WAVE WAVE
Bye-bye.
Whoa.
You sure have a MESSY FACE.
And HANDS.
I think it's time for a BABY BATH!
Quack!

Hey! Come back!
No!
Hold still!
No!
Be a good baby!
No!

But you've got a MESSY FACE!
No!
No!
No!

Meanwhile, we am GLORK PATROLLING.
Yes, we are!
It am FUN!
And I'm SO GOOD at it!
Just LOOK at me!
But be CAREFUL. Glork Patrol am fun but can also be DANGERISH.
Dangerous?
But I'm so BIG and STRONG!

Whoa!
Look at this GIANT HOLE!
See? Me told you so...
DANGERISH.
If my Da-da was here he would fall RIGHT IN.

But I'm NOT HIM!
I have a SUPER ROBO-SUIT!
And I...
CAN JUMP!
Right OVER!

Meanwhile, Gloo Gloo is walking with Momma!
Tra-la-la!
BLARG!
Look OUT!

Eek!
POP!
WHAM
What happened to Gloo Gloo?
Glork Patrol just SAVED your LIFE!

You almost stepped in a BIG HOLE!
See?
Wow!
Scary!
Stay away from the edge, Gloo Gloo!
SNATCH!
Oh, Glork Patrol! Thank you for saving my little Gloo Gloo!
How can I ever REPAY you?

No pay.
We happy just to do VICTORY POSE.
Right?
Victory pose?
Yeah, like THIS!
TA-DA!
POP

THUMP
Eeek!
My ARM popped OFF!
Oh my!
Eeek!
My OTHER arm!
DROP

What's happening to me?
What's happening to my ROBO-SUIT?
PEEL
PEEL
Uh-oh...
Maybe we am big SILLIES to make the WHOLE THING from CANDY WRAPPERS.
And gum.
FLOOP
Oh, floop.

POOF
Oh No! You fall down!
Super Backpack, am you okay?
Yes.
Actually, I feel GREAT!
That was the most FUN I ever had!

Oh, phew!
That am GOOD NEWS!
Hey!
Me think it am time...
...for a VICTORY POSE!
Ha ha!
TA-DA!

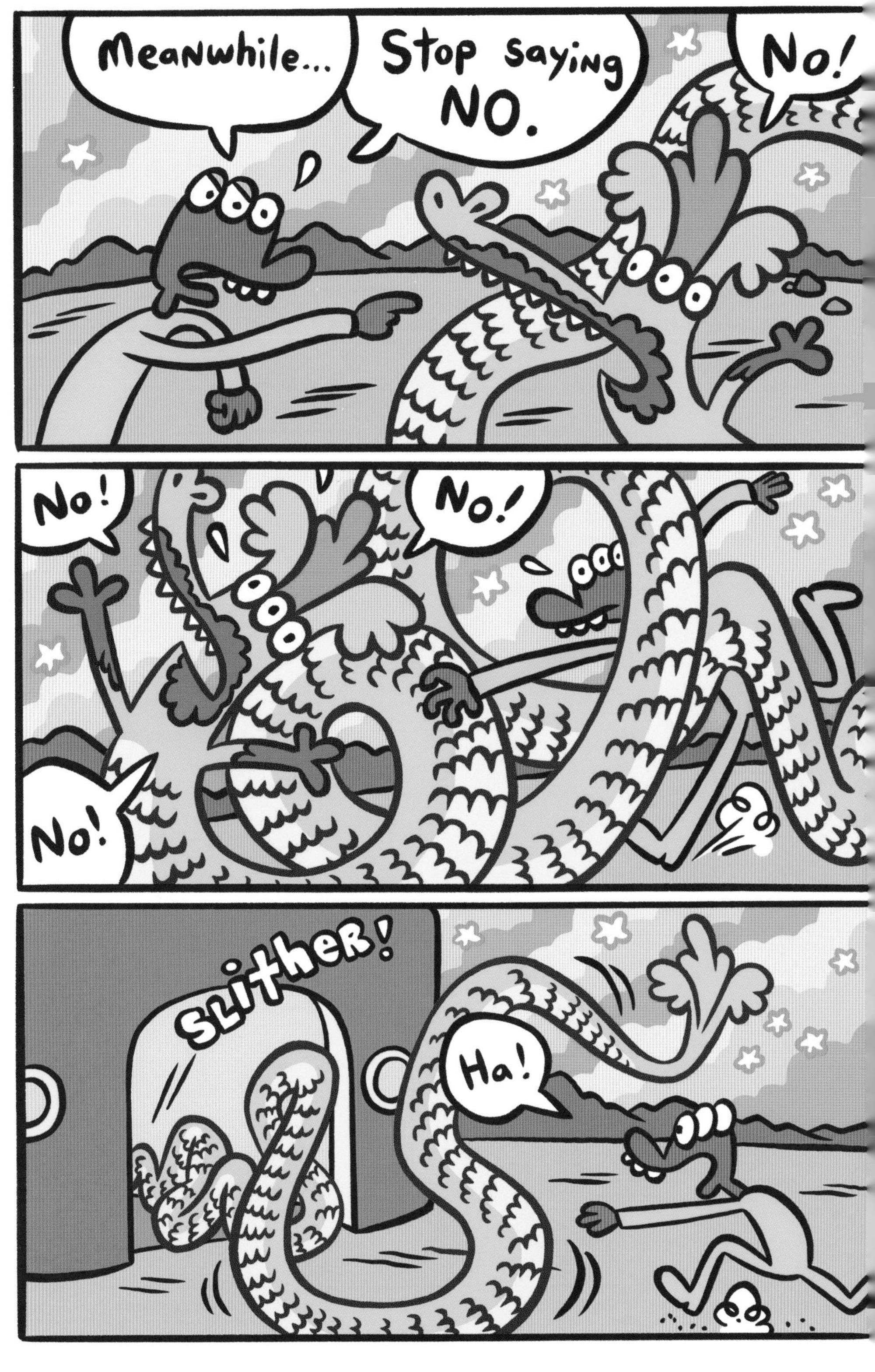
Meanwhile...
Stop saying NO.
No!
No!
No!
No!
SLITHER!
Ha!

Now I've got you cornered!
Get Ready for-
CRASH!
-bath time?
NOOooo!
CRASH!

Meanwhile, we am walking home!
Yeah!
Walk, walk, walk!
Look.
A chunk of stuff.
And another, and another.
And another!

Hey! what happened to GLORK BASE?!

Peek!

Baby Quackaboodle?!

She had her first bath... and guess what?
Quack!
She LOVED it!
Time for another VICTORY POSE!
Ta-da!
THE END